This book belongs to

Alkokab Publications
96 Morley Road
London E10 6LL

www.alkokab.com

ISBN 978-0-9554302-0-6

Design & Art Direction
Ilham Imtiaze Ahmed

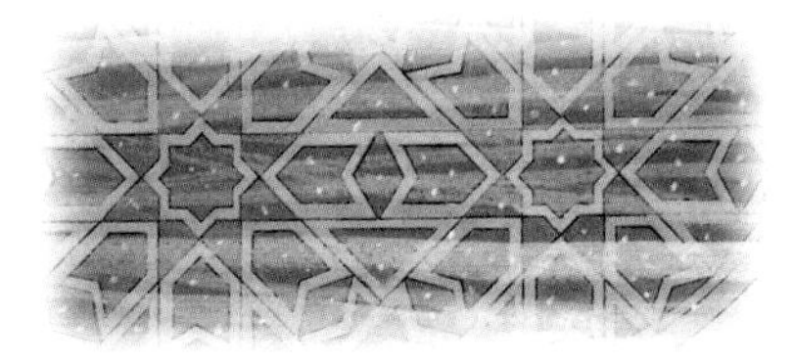

Eid a Poem

Asma Ahmad

It was the night before Eid, when all through the house,

Everybody was busy, rushing about.

All the doors were flung open and lights switched on,

Bedtime was ignored — so much had to be done.

Mamma was in the kitchen making some treats,

Papa was tidying and making things neat,

Big sister Aliya was mending her scarf,

While big brother Adil was having a bath.

The twins were jumping up and down on their beds,
When they should have been cleaning their room instead.
On the floor lay their clothes waiting to be pressed,
So that on the morrow they would be well-dressed.

Then twin one fell down hard and began to howl,

Ma was cross and shouted, 'Not another sound!'

Quietly everyone completed their tasks,

And as the clock struck twelve, all went to bed fast.

Near the front door, coats had been hung with great care,

And shoes had been shone and placed ready to wear.

And everyone was now fast away sleeping,

And it was of Eid-day that they were dreaming.

The clock ticked on and fajr time swiftly dawned,
Papa's alarm began to buzz and he yawned,
His eyes flickered, but then he slept on some more!
Mamma jumped up when papa gave a loud snore!

She looked at the time and shouted: ‘wake up all!’
And all fell out of bed at mamma’s loud call.
One after the other wudu they all made,
And salatul fajr they all calmly prayed.

Twin one then decided to go back to sleep,
When twin two reminded him today was Eid,
Excitement began to fill everyone's heart,
And all began to get ready to depart.

To the masjid quickly they all made their way,

Twin one forgot his hat causing slight delay.

All around them people were going to work,

The twins were glad that today school they could shirk.

They arrived just in time for the Eid prayer,

Aliya stood beside her friend Sumayya.

Many people had crammed into the masjid,

And after salat, each other they greeted.

Twin one and twin two did with their friends play games,

Aliya with Sumayya did just the same,

Mamma sat down to catch up with all her friends,

Papa to serving tea and snacks did attend.

From the grownups the children received money,

And after midday dinner the kids hurried

To the shops to buy themselves all kinds of treats.

The twins did buy toy cars and some sticky sweets.

In the evening cousins did come round to play,

The twins did persuade them to all night long stay,

They planned not to sleep, but all were too dozy,

To run around all night long and be noisy.

After isha not a creature was stirring,

All though the house, all the people were snoring,

All the doors were closed shut and off were the lights,

Outside, up in the dark sky, the moon shone bright.